Courage to Ride

Bernadette Kelly

Courage to Ride

Bernadette Kelly

Raintree is an imprint of Capstone Global Library Limited,
a company incorporated in England and Wales having its
registered office at 7 Pilgrim Street, London, EC4V 6LB –
Registered company number: 6695582

To contact Raintree, please phone 0845 6044371, fax +44 (0)1865 312263,
or email myorders@raintreepublishers.co.uk.

First published in Australia by Black Dog Books in 2006
Copyright © Bernadette Kelly 2006
First published in the United Kingdom in 2014
The moral rights of the proprietor have been asserted.

Editor: Diyan Leake
Art Director: Kay Fraser
Graphic Designer: Emily Harris
Production Specialist: Michelle Biedscheid
Originated by Capstone Global Library Ltd
Printed and bound in China

Main cover photograph reproduced with permission
of Shutterstock (© R. Carner). Background image reproduced with
permission of Shutterstock (© Dhoxax).

ISBN 978 1 406 26670 2
17 16 15 14 13
10 9 8 7 6 5 4 3 2 1

British Library Cataloguing in Publication Data
A full catalogue record for this book is available from the British Library.

"Bobby, you have no manners," I said with a giggle. I loved the way my horse gobbled his apple treats. I didn't even mind when the foamy apple juice dribbled off his muzzle on to my hands and made them all sticky.

Some mornings I would wake up thinking that maybe I'd dreamed my new life. A life in the country. A life with my very own horse.

I had wanted a horse for as long as I could remember, but the city was no place to keep one. Then my father was offered a job in the town of Ridgeview, and my family relocated to the country.

I had been nervous about moving away from the only home I'd ever known. I missed city life – especially my best friend, Jade O'Brien.

The only good thing about moving to the country was the possibility of getting a horse. But my father decided having a horse was too much trouble. It was only when a neighbour, Mrs Cameron, gave me a horse named Bobby that my father finally changed his mind about letting me have a horse.

I loved everything about Bobby. I could spend hours watching him. He would often come up to me at the gate and nudge me, searching for the apple I always carried.

Bobby was funny. He loved to annoy my dad's six sheep, which shared the field with him. Much to my father's annoyance, Bobby bossed those sheep about like an overgrown sheep dog.

But I wanted much more than to just watch Bobby in the field. I wanted to ride him. And for that, I needed tack.

"I'm off to look at some tack, boy," I said with one last stroke of his soft muzzle. "You and I have some serious riding to do."

* * *

"Hello? Anyone here?" I called. I stepped into my neighbour's large barn and breathed in the most wonderful mix of smells.

The heavy aroma of leather hung in the air. The fresh smell of hay wafted from the back of the room.

Gold and green bales of hay and straw were stacked to the roof against the back wall. In front of the hay were a couple of plastic feed bins and some freestanding shelves holding grooming equipment, hoof picks, and bottles of horse shampoo. A couple of halters and a bridle were hanging off hooks on the wall beside saddles on racks.

"Hey, Annie. I'm glad you made it. This is Jake," said my neighbour, and new friend, Reese Moriarty. "Jake is the person I wanted you to meet," she added. "I thought you might want to talk to him about buying some tack for Bobby."

"Hello, Annie," said Mrs Moriarty with a smile.

"Hi, Mrs Moriarty. Hello, Jake," I said, a little shyly.

Jake nodded. "Hi. You must be new in town," he said. Then he smiled at me. "Am I gaining another customer?" he asked. "Are you in the market for some tack?"

"Maybe," I replied.

"Come on. Let's get the rest unloaded," said Reese impatiently. "Just wait till you see what Jake's got in the back of his van."

Reese was my only friend in Ridgeview, and the word *friend* was probably stretching things. I hoped I would meet more people when school began. So far, I only knew Reese and some of the other riders I'd met at Ridgeview Riding Club.

I liked Reese, but she had a way of making me feel... well, stupid. She just seemed to know so much – about horses, about the countryside, about everything.

I helped unload the bags while Reese explained what was going on.

"Ridgeview and the other towns in the area don't have a tack shop, so Jake travels around with his van packed with gear. Jefferson needs a new blanket. I thought you might need some things for Bobby," Reese told me.

"Bobby?" said Jake. "Is that your horse's name, Annie?"

"Yes," I said, smiling, still not quite believing my luck.

I helped carry in the plastic bags from the van. There were saddles and bridles, blankets of various styles and fabrics, brushes, bandages, saddlecloths – it looked like Jake's Travelling Tack Shop had it all.

This was good news for me. I needed more than one or two things for Bobby. I needed everything. When Mrs Cameron had handed Bobby over, it had been with a halter and a lead and nothing else.

Jake lined everything up for us to see. My eyes fell on a black leather saddle with a deep, comfortable-looking seat.

I reached out and touched the flap. I loved the soft feel of it.

"Reese – this is it. This is the saddle I want," I said. "It's exactly right."

Reese was unfolding blankets with her mother. She dropped the one she was holding and walked over to the black saddle.

She whistled softly. "Only the best, huh?" She grabbed the attached tag and flipped it over to see the price. She raised her eyebrows and lifted the tag a little so I could see. The price on the tag was two and a half thousand pounds.

I frowned. Even if one of the zeros magically disappeared, I knew my parents would never pay that kind of money for a saddle.

"Annie, that's not what you need, anyway," Reese told me. "This is a dressage saddle. See the way the flaps are cut?" She pointed to the leather flaps where a rider's leg would rest. The sides were long and straight.

"What's the difference?" I asked.

"If you want to ride at the riding club you'll need an all-purpose saddle," said Reese.

I really wanted to join the riding club. It looked like fun. Reese had urged me to join the club, so I had applied to become a member.

"Dressage saddles help your leg position by keeping it long and straight, but you need a saddle for jumping, too," continued Reese. "An all-purpose saddle has the flaps cut more forward. It's supposed to be, like, in between – designed for dressage and jumping. You want to learn how to jump with Bobby, don't you?"

"Of course I want to jump," I said quickly, although my stomach flipped over at the thought. I wasn't sure what dressage meant either, but I was too embarrassed to ask.

Reese grinned. "Maybe you should worry about learning to ride first. Here, what about this one? It's pretty nice, and it's much cheaper."

She pointed to another black saddle. At first I couldn't see any difference between it and my first choice, but when I looked more closely I could see that Reese was right. The flaps were cut differently. There were other small differences, too. The seat and the kneepads were made of suede, and the leather was shinier.

I checked the price and sighed. Eight hundred pounds. That was still too much. I needed a saddle and a bridle, grooming equipment, a safety helmet, riding boots – the list seemed endless. I would never convince my mum and dad to let me spend so much money. And the birthday money I had saved wouldn't stretch far.

"See anything you like?" asked Jake.

"Lots," I said. "But nothing I can afford."

"That's too bad," he said. "Have you tried looking in the newspaper for some secondhand stuff?"

"Secondhand?" I repeated. "But I wanted to get new things!"

Jake frowned. "How long have you been riding?" he asked.

I dropped my eyes. "I can't actually ride," I said. "But I'm going to learn. Just as soon as I get some tack."

"Then take some free advice from me," he said kindly. "You could spend thousands of pounds buying the very best gear, and I'd love to sell it to you. But isn't it better to start out with secondhand gear than no gear at all? I guarantee your horse won't care if the saddle is new or old, as long as it fits him comfortably."

I scuffed my boot on the ground. Jake's suggestion made sense, but now that I had my horse, I wanted to show him off to the world. I didn't want to look like a beginner, even if I really was one.

"Looks like I don't have a choice," I muttered.

Chapter Two

When I got home, I grabbed a muesli bar and the local paper and sat down in the kitchen with my dog, Jonesy, at my feet. Scanning the classified section, I read through the list of items for sale.

These ads were nothing like the ones in city papers. There were cows for sale, hay, even an ad for a tractor, but no tack.

As I scanned through the paper again, my mother came in, wearing gardening gloves.

"My goodness, it's warm outside." Mum wiped her forearm across her brow. "What's up, sweetie?"

I took a deep breath. "Could I have my birthday money early?" I asked.

My mother frowned. "Annie, your birthday is ten months away," she said. "What do you need money for?"

"I can't ride Bobby without tack, and I don't have money to buy any," I told her.

"I know," said my mother. "I talked about this with your father. We agreed to put aside three hundred pounds so that you can get yourself a saddle and bridle for Bobby."

"Three hundred pounds?" I cried. Then I saw the frown on my mother's face. "I mean, I looked in the paper for secondhand tack, but there's nothing that cheap. I'm probably going to have to buy some new stuff."

Mum rummaged through a pile of papers on the kitchen worktop. She pulled out a newspaper clipping.

"I saw this ad in last week's paper," she said, uncrumpling the piece of paper. "Someone is selling the whole package. The ad says there's a saddle, bridle, grooming equipment, and riding helmet. There's even a secondhand saddle blanket. All for two hundred and eighty-five pounds."

It's probably horrible, I thought glumly.

* * *

Later on, Mum and I drove to an area of small farms only a few minutes from our own home. The property was on a quiet, leafy street. The house was large, with a tree-lined driveway and fields on both sides. Hope rose in my chest. These people looked rich. Maybe the secondhand tack wouldn't be bad after all.

A woman came to greet us in the yard. She looked kind of familiar to me.

She looks rich, I thought.

That's when it hit me – the woman was Mrs Coulson, Jessica Coulson's mother!

I had met Jessica and her mother at the riding club right after I moved to Ridgeview. I thought Jessica was a spoiled brat. She was the only person who hadn't been at all nice to me. The last thing I wanted to do was to buy Jessica's secondhand tack. There was no way I could handle the embarrassment.

"Mum," I said quickly. "I changed my mind. Let's go."

My mother stared at me. "What? I thought you wanted tack to ride Bobby."

"I do," I said. "But maybe we should look somewhere else."

Mum frowned. "Annie, don't be silly. We're here now. We are going to look at this tack. It sounds just right. Come on."

My mother stepped out of the car and talked to Mrs Coulson, who led us around the side of the house. I followed unhappily. Mrs Coulson hadn't recognized me. Maybe I'd get lucky and I wouldn't bump into Jessica.

Everything in the Coulsons' tack room was locked neatly away in the cabinets that lined the walls. The only things not stashed away were an old saddle and a few other pieces of tack in a lonely pile on the floor.

I guessed that it was the tack for sale. The saddle was nothing like the beautiful black one I'd first spied at Reese's. The seat was old and scratched, and the suede on the kneepads had long since been rubbed away.

The bridle was old, too. It looked hard and brittle, not soft like the beautiful bridles that Jake had been selling. There was also a grubby blue saddle blanket that was fraying around the edges, a grungy riding helmet, and two grooming brushes. Even the brushes were old-looking, with broken handles and worn bristles.

"Well, here is the gear," said Mrs Coulson. "It's pretty worn, but I think you're getting a bargain."

"I don't –" I began.

"It looks fine," said Mum, gathering up the gear. "We'll take it. You're all set now, Annie. Just think! You'll be riding that horse before you know it."

Mrs Coulson smiled as Mum piled gear into my arms.

I would be smiling, too, I thought, *if I had just sold a pile of old junk for two hundred and eighty-five pounds.*

"You know, Ridgeview has a good riding club. My daughter rides there. Your daughter should go down some time and take a look," Mrs Coulson told Mum.

I didn't bother telling Mrs Coulson that I'd already applied to join. It was becoming clear to me that deciding to join the club had been one of my stupidest ideas ever.

Now I would have to show up at the riding club with Jessica Coulson's hand-me-downs.

When we got home, I tied Bobby to the base of a tree in the backyard. The rope was long enough for Bobby to nibble at the grass on the lawn. The secondhand tack lay on the ground nearby.

Now that I had the tack, I wasn't exactly sure what to do with it. The saddle looked easy enough, but the bridle was a mess. I stared down at a confusing number of straps. They all seemed to be attached to the metal bit.

I tried to figure it out, but the only thing I knew for sure was that the bit went in the horse's mouth.

Mrs Moriarty pulled up in her large 4×4. She slammed the door behind her and walked towards my house, dragging a large bag with one hand and holding an envelope in the other.

"Hello, Annie," she said. "I see you found some tack. Come inside for a minute, okay? I have some good news."

I left the tack on the ground and followed Mrs Moriarty into the house.

"Susan," called Mrs Moriarty cheerfully once she was inside the kitchen. "Do you have any fresh coffee?"

"I do," my mum yelled back. "Be there in a minute. I just made the coffee in the kitchen five minutes ago."

Mrs Moriarty and my mother had become good friends. My mother could make friends wherever she was.

I must take after my father, I thought.

My mum walked in and hugged Mrs Moriarty. "What brings you here?" she asked.

Mrs Moriarty smiled and said, "I just wanted to say congratulations to the newest Ridgeview Riding Club member. Annie, here's your official acceptance." Mrs Moriarty handed me the white envelope. "I'm on the committee, so I offered to personally deliver the good news."

I tore open the envelope. I was so excited, I could hardly see the words on the paper. There was something about welcoming a new member and an account for the fees.

Mrs Moriarty pointed to the bag she'd brought in from her car. "These clothes are for you," she said. "Reese outgrew them – I think she's a little taller than you. Go ahead, try them on."

I escaped to my room, realizing too late that I'd rudely forgotten to thank Mrs Moriarty.

I dumped the bag out on my floor. The pile of clothes included a jumper in the Ridgeview Riding Club colours, a club tie, and a white shirt and jodhpurs.

Great, I thought bitterly. Secondhand tack. Secondhand uniform. Could things get any worse?

I tried on the uniform and checked out my reflection in my full-length mirror. The jumper would last a while, but the jodhpurs were a little tight. The shirt fit well, but I wasn't sure what to do with the tie. I took off the uniform, threw it on my bed, and dressed in my own clothes again.

"Aren't you going to model for us?" Mrs Moriarty sounded disappointed when I returned to the kitchen.

I avoided her eyes. "Oh, no," I said. "It fits really well. Thanks, Mrs Moriarty." I quickly changed the subject, "So, how's Reese?"

"She's out riding, of course. I was just telling your mother you should come over with your new horse," Mrs Moriarty told me. "I'm sure Reese would love to give you a lesson – as long as you show up this time."

Mrs Moriarty chuckled, but I blushed. Reese had offered to give me a lesson once before on her horse, Jefferson, but I had stood her up. I still wasn't sure that Reese had forgiven me.

"If it's not too much trouble… " I began.

"I'll tell her to call you."

An angry yell from outside filtered through to the kitchen.

"Annie!" It was my father.

I realized that I'd left Bobby tied to the tree. "Gotta go," I called as I raced through the back door in a panic.

Chaos greeted me outside. Bobby had somehow got loose from the tree. The rope trailed behind him as he wandered across the lawn, snatching grass and chewing as he went. My father was standing over the tack that I'd left on the ground.

"Is this the way you treat your things, young lady?" he growled. "Your mother and I spent good money on this gear, and look where you left it. That horse could have trampled all over it."

"Okay, okay," I muttered quietly.

I ran to catch Bobby, but I couldn't. I only managed to frighten my poor horse when I ran at him. He turned and trotted back across the lawn, lifting his tail and leaving a long trail of droppings as he went.

Just then, my dog, Jonesy, picked up the chase and began yapping at Bobby's heels. Bobby headed down the driveway with me in hot pursuit and my father yelling after me.

Bobby didn't run far. He found a patch of grass just outside the field gate and stopped to sample it. I grabbed the rope and led him back into the field, but the damage had been done.

My father hadn't wanted a horse. He could still change his mind and return Bobby to Mrs Cameron. I would have to be more careful.

Bobby didn't know it, but as far as my father was concerned, my horse was on borrowed time.

Every time I thought about riding Bobby, I felt a little odd. Just the thought of sitting on his back made my stomach feel like it was full of galloping horses.

After that first amazing day, when Mrs Cameron had delivered Bobby to our house, I had spent most of my time just hanging on the gate to his field, watching him.

Now that I had tack, there was no excuse not to ride Bobby. I had spent my whole life dreaming about owning a horse and learning to ride. Now that the dream was becoming a reality, I knew I should be thrilled.

Instead, I was panicking. What if I turned out to be a horrible rider?

When Reese called later that day, she seemed grumpier than usual. "I heard that my mother told you I would give you a riding lesson."

"I'd love that," I said. I hesitated. It didn't sound as if Reese was very excited about the idea. "Only if you want to, though," I added quickly.

There was a silence on the end of the line. When Reese spoke again, she sounded slightly less grumpy. "You can bring Bobby over this afternoon at two. Have him saddled, but lead him. Don't try to ride. See you then."

"I won't be late," I said.

But Reese had already hung up.

* * *

Unfortunately, I was late for my riding
lesson.

"Sorry I'm late," I told Reese when I finally
arrived at half past two that afternoon.

Bobby was walking along behind me, but
he wasn't happy about it. My dog, Jonesy, had
come for the walk. In the short time it took to
walk next door to Reese's house, the little dog
had made a nuisance of himself. He'd run
ahead, then dart between Bobby's legs and
dodge a couple of angry kicks from the horse.

"It took me longer than I thought it would
to get Bobby tacked up," I said, trying to
explain.

Reese frowned when she glanced at Bobby's
saddle and bridle. "You should have taken
more time," she said. "The girth is way too
loose. Your bridle is twisted, and the bit is in

his mouth the wrong way. Mum told me you found some secondhand gear. Why did you buy a dressage saddle?"

I looked at my saddle. "My parents bought it for me," I said quietly.

"Well, I guess it'll have to work. At your level it probably won't matter anyway." Reese turned to Jonesy. "Why is he here?"

Reese wasn't crazy about Jonesy. The first time Reese had met him, the dog had chased and frightened Reese's horse, Jefferson. Reese may have forgiven, but she had obviously not forgotten.

"He won't get into trouble," I said. "He just wants to watch."

But Reese bent down and grabbed Jonesy's collar. "The last thing you need as a beginner is a crazy dog yapping at your horse's heels," she told me.

Reese dragged Jonesy across the yard. She opened the shed door, pushed the little dog inside, and closed the door. One muffled bark was heard from inside the shed, and then silence.

I felt like grabbing my dog and horse and going back home. "Hey!" I said angrily.

Reese crossed her arms and raised an eyebrow at me. "He'll be fine. I'm just keeping him out of trouble, that's all. Come on, let's get started."

While I was deciding whether to stay or not, Reese began her lesson.

"This gear needs to be oiled," said Reese, running her hands across the leather seat of the saddle.

I fumbled with what seemed like endless buckles and straps, getting everything set up. Then the galloping horses started up again in my stomach when Reese helped me up on to Bobby's back.

After Bobby had walked around in circles for ten minutes, my nerves began to settle. "I'm ready to trot now," I told Reese.

"No, you're not," said Reese firmly. "If you don't get the walk right, you won't have a chance of mastering the trot. If you want to ride properly, it's important to take things slowly." I wanted to tell her I could do it, but instead I kept quiet, trying to avoid an argument.

Reese wasn't a very patient teacher. "Heels down, Annie. Shoulders back. You are slouching, Annie. SIT UP STRAIGHT!"

After walking around in circles for an hour, I felt awful. I was supposed to go to the riding club on Sunday. It was Thursday, and I couldn't even trot yet.

When it was time to go, Reese let Jonesy out of the shed. I was about to ride home, but Reese insisted I get off Bobby's back and lead him.

"Don't ride him on your own. You're not ready for that yet," she told me. "You can come back on Saturday for another lesson."

Back at home, I untacked Bobby. Then I brushed his coat until it gleamed, speaking softly to him as I worked.

"That was so boring," I murmured. "I'll never learn to ride if we stick to Reese's schedule. I think we need to speed things up, don't you?"

* * *

That evening at dinner I told my parents about my lesson with Reese. I tried to make the lesson sound as exciting as possible as I described what I'd learned.

"She's going to give me another lesson on Saturday," I said after I'd told them all about the lesson. "And I thought I'd take Bobby out for a ride in the woods tomorrow."

My father lowered his fork. "That's not a good idea," he said. "It's not safe."

"Your dad's right, Annie," agreed my mother. "You should wait until Saturday when Reese can help you."

I stared at my parents. What was the big deal? I was tired of being treated like a baby.

We'll see, I thought. *We'll just see.*

Chapter
Five

The next afternoon I saddled up Bobby on my own.

I pushed down an uneasy feeling. My parents hadn't actually forbidden me to go riding, had they? No. So I was fine.

I struggled with the bridle, but eventually managed to get it over Bobby's ears and buckled up. I hoped it was right.

My first problem was mounting the horse. Without Reese to help me by giving me a leg up, I had to find something that I could stand on.

I scanned the yard, but the only thing I could see was an old plastic bucket. I turned it upside down, led Bobby into position beside the bucket, and stepped up on to it.

Before I had a chance to do anything else, I felt myself slowly sinking. As the bucket caved in, my feet slipped off and I landed square on my bottom.

"Ouch!" I yelled.

Bobby stared down at me on the ground. The horse's big dark eyes seemed puzzled, as if he was wondering what on earth his silly owner was up to.

Cautiously rubbing my bottom, I decided to try something else. After thinking about it for a minute, I settled on trying Reese's way of mounting with the stirrup.

Holding the saddle for balance, I lifted my left foot and pushed it into the stirrup. I hung awkwardly for a moment, with one leg raised high in the air and the other hopping to keep from falling backwards. Then I pushed my weight into the stirrup and jumped up with the right leg, in an effort to swing it over the saddle.

It was at this exact moment that Bobby decided to take a step forward. He moved just far enough for me to miss the saddle and swing on to his round rump, which I immediately slid off.

This time I landed on my feet. Embarrassed, I quickly looked around to make sure that no one was watching.

This was ridiculous. At the riding club, everyone had swung easily into their saddles, even the little kids in the junior group. I wanted to give up. But I knew I couldn't.

Before trying again, I took both reins and held them firmly in one hand to hold Bobby and keep him from moving.

"Easy, boy," I murmured.

My third attempt became a hasty scramble when Bobby stepped forward again, but this time I managed to cling to his mane and hoist myself up.

"We did it," I told the horse, lightly stroking his neck. "It's probably not supposed to be so hard, though," I added quietly.

Then I heard a bark. Jonesy was in the field. He'd chased one of the sheep away from the rest and was cheerfully nipping its heels as it tried to escape.

"Stupid sheep," I said, before slipping off Bobby's back and calling the dog.

I'd forgotten to put Jonesy in his kennel. Even without his sheep-chasing ways, I would have had to leave him behind. Otherwise he could get lost in the woods.

It took another twenty minutes for me to shut Jonesy in his kennel. Then, after a couple of unsuccessful attempts, I finally climbed back into the saddle.

"Great," I told Bobby. "Come on. Let's go have some fun."

I was getting sick of riding around in circles. Bobby and I were going for a real ride. Guiding with the reins, I turned Bobby to the driveway.

Since moving to Ridgeview, I had explored my new neighbourhood with Jonesy at my side. The dog didn't appreciate being left behind. He whined mournfully and scratched at the kennel door.

I urged Bobby towards the nearby country park. Once we were on the bridle path, the trees closed around us like a cool, shady cocoon. The only sound to break the peace was an occasional birdcall.

For a while, Bobby and I went along at a walk, but I really wanted to try trotting. In the horse stories I'd read, the riders always seemed to be kicking at the horses' sides. How hard could it be?

I nudged Bobby's sides with my knees. "Okay, Bobby. Come on, boy. Let's go," I urged. "Faster!"

The horse ignored me and kept walking. I sighed.

I thought back to my lesson with Reese. When Reese wanted me to ask Bobby to walk, she'd told me to give him a little kick. If a little kick was the signal for walk, maybe a big kick would make Bobby go faster.

I pushed my legs back behind the saddle and whacked my heels against Bobby's flanks.

The poor horse was so startled that he lunged forward with fright, then took off at a canter for a half dozen strides.

Unprepared, I was instantly thrown off balance. My feet left the stirrups and I slid sideways. Bobby slowed down, but it was too late.

Gravity took over and I landed on my side in the long grass on the side of the road. For a moment, I lay still. Bobby, now calm again, grazed not far away from me.

I heard muffled hoof-beats. As the sound drew closer along the bridle path, I groaned and stood up carefully. I checked each limb for pain.

"Nothing broken," I muttered with a shaky laugh that ended in a sob.

I quickly hobbled over and grabbed Bobby's reins. Whoever was coming down the bridle

path might be able to help me get back on. I
led Bobby back on to the bridle path – straight
into the path of Reese and Jefferson.

"What happened?" Reese asked coldly,
looking me up and down.

I didn't say anything. I just brushed the dirt
from my knees and removed a twig from my
hair.

"Did you fall off?" asked Reese.

I nodded.

"Is Bobby all right?" asked Reese.

"Yeah, and I'm fine, too," I said angrily. Hot
tears prickled my eyelids.

"I told you not to ride alone, "Reese said,
shaking her head.

"I was just taking Bobby for a walk!" I
argued.

"Annie, Bobby could have been injured. Really badly. And you could've got really hurt," Reese added. "But obviously you know better. You don't need my help."

Reese clicked her tongue and turned Jefferson. I was left standing on the bridle path, watching Jefferson's silvery tail disappear from view as he cantered away.

By the time I had walked Bobby home, I'd replayed my meeting with Reese fifty times.

The problem with new friends is that you never know where you stand with them. Suddenly, I really wanted to hear Jade's voice. My old friend would love me no matter what. As soon as I got inside, I called her number.

Jade's mother picked up when I called. "Hi, Annie!" she said happily. "It's nice to hear from you."

I politely answered Mrs O'Brien's questions: how did I like living in the country? How were my mum and dad? But when I asked to speak to Jade, Mrs O'Brien was apologetic.

"I'm sorry, Annie, she's not here. She went ice skating with a couple of girls from school," she told me.

I put the phone down slowly. Ice skating! Jade and I would sometimes go ice skating at the fancy rink near the shopping centre. But in a country town like Ridgeview, ice skating wasn't an option.

I spent a sleepless night thinking about the day's events. I just kept getting angrier and angrier.

Who did Reese think she was? Bobby was my horse. I could do what I wanted with him. Besides, I was fine, and so was Bobby. Nothing bad had happened.

But what if things hadn't worked out so well? What if Bobby had been hurt?

I had promised Mrs Cameron that I would take care of him. It was my job to keep him safe. My actions had put both me and Bobby in danger.

In the morning, before I had time to chicken out, I called Reese.

"Hi, it's Annie," I said when she answered the phone.

"Oh," Reese said quietly.

"Reese, you were absolutely right," I told her. "I wanted to speed things up. It's just that I've wanted this for so long. I just want to be able to do everything right away. I bet you think I'm stupid."

"Annie – I get it. Really. It just doesn't work that way!" she said.

"I know. I promise to listen to everything you say. Can I please have another lesson before the riding club rally?" I asked quietly.

"Sure," Reese said. "See you tomorrow?"

"Yes!" I said, relieved. "Thanks, Reese. You won't regret it."

* * *

My second lesson went much better than the first. Reese showed me how to squeeze Bobby's sides with my calves when I wanted him to increase his gait from a walk to a trot.

I soon realized that he was willing to go faster for me, without any sudden jerky forward movements that left me unseated. This time, I listened to Reese's advice and took things slowly.

Sunday was riding club day. I normally hated early mornings – especially at the weekend. But today was different. I jumped out of bed before my alarm clock went off, quickly ate some toast, and headed outside.

Reese's mother had offered to take both Bobby and Jefferson in the horse trailer, but Reese wanted me to take a warm-up ride before the rally. We decided to ride through the country park on a narrow bridle path that led right into the town of Ridgeview.

The riding club grounds were located on the edge of town, right beside the racecourse. Reese's mum had promised to meet us there with buckets and hay bags for the horses and the trailer to bring them home.

It had rained overnight and the road outside my house was wet and muddy. Tiny brown puddles dotted the road's surface. I heard Reese's horse clopping around the corner before I could see him. Reese, dressed in her riding club uniform, waved and pushed Jefferson into a trot.

"Sorry I'm late," said Reese. "We should really get going if we want to make gear check on time."

We headed down the road. The horses' hooves splashed tiny sprays of mud as we rode along.

Travelling through the silent woods at such an early hour was a whole new experience for me. I had spent hours walking through it with Jonesy, but today every sense seemed sharper. Twigs cracked sharply beneath the horses' feet. Moisture from last night's rain dripped steadily from every leaf.

Jefferson peered around nervously, alert to every noise in the trees. Bobby walked behind. He was calmer, but still produced an occasional uneasy snort.

There was a sudden crazy flapping as a startled bird flew out of the undergrowth beside the path.

Jefferson, already tense, stopped sharply and spun around 180 degrees. Bobby, close behind, was shoved sideways.

For the second time in only a few days, I found myself sitting on the ground. Unhurt, I leaped to my feet. But I wasn't quick enough to save my uniform, which was covered in slimy brown mud.

"That's what you get for riding so close!" Reese snapped. "That wasn't poor Jefferson's fault. He had nowhere to go. We're lucky one of the horses isn't hurt." She shook her head. Then she added, "Are you okay?"

"I'm fine. But we'll have to turn around so I can change," I said.

Reese shook her head. "There's no time. We'll probably be late as it is. Besides, you don't have a spare uniform. Let the mud dry and we can brush it off when we get there."

I remounted and we took off again. I was mad at myself for falling off and ruining my uniform. I would definitely be the centre of attention today, but for all the wrong reasons.

As if she could tell I was upset, Reese suddenly said, "Don't worry about it. It's part of riding. Even experienced riders fall off – just not as often."

"But what about gear check?" I said. I felt tears prick my eyelids. "I'm a mess."

Reese giggled suddenly. "Yes, you are. Don't get near Jessica – you'll give her a heart attack."

Jessica Coulson, ex-owner of my secondhand tack. Jessica Coulson, owner of a prize show horse and fashion queen of the riding club with her expensive gloves and helmet and perfect riding club uniform. I imagined rubbing mud on to Jessica. It was a pretty funny image.

I started to laugh. By the time we rode out of the woods, I had cheered up a bit. I was looking forward to the day.

We rode past rows of cars and horse trailers lined up in the parking lot. We reached Reese's group, where Mrs Mason, the district commissioner, had already begun the gear check.

I smiled a greeting at Matt Snyder, Austin Ryan, and of course, Jessica. The riders were watching me with weird looks on their faces. Austin was smirking. Too late, I remembered the state of my uniform.

Reese stepped in to explain. "You all remember Annie, don't you? She fell off on the way here," she said bluntly.

I was mortified. Jessica chose that moment to recognize my tack. "Hey," she said loudly. "Were you the one who bought that pile of old stuff from our tack shed?"

"I have no idea," I answered airily. "My mother bought this stuff, not me."

Jessica sniffed. "That's funny. Mum told me there was a woman and a girl –"

Matt cut in. "My dad said your horse has been to the riding club before."

"Really?" I said in surprise.

"Yep," Matt replied. "Dad said Bobby could teach you a thing or two. Bobby could probably teach the whole group."

I glanced at Jessica and saw her lift one eyebrow as if she didn't believe a word of it.

Well, I thought. *We'll show her, won't we, Bobby – I hope.*

Chapter Eight

Everybody mounted and rode across the grounds to the dressage area. The first lesson was with Erica. I was still puzzled by the word *dressage* and finally got the courage to ask Reese what it meant. Reese looked annoyed, but she answered patiently. "Dressage means training. It's a test of horse and rider and how well they can work together. Come on, we better get over there."

As we rode, Jessica moved up beside me. "What breed is your horse?" she asked.

Jessica said the word *horse* as if she was talking about a disease. And judging by the way she was sneering at Bobby, I could tell she didn't think much of him.

"I don't know," I answered honestly. "The lady who gave him to me didn't say."

"She gave him away? I'm not surprised. I guess she didn't want him," said Jessica.

I told myself I didn't care what Jessica thought. I tried not to compare my scruffy, long-eared Bobby to Jessica's sleek show horse, Ripple.

Jessica sniffed. "Well, at least he's clean," she said, looking at my muddy uniform. "Are you going to clip out his ears?"

What was Jessica talking about? I didn't have a clue. "Huh?"

"Bobby. Are you going to clip his ears?" Jessica asked again.

"Why would I do that?" I was genuinely puzzled.

Jessica snorted. "Why wouldn't you? I mean, look at them. There are clumps of hair sticking out of them. It's... ugly."

Jessica was too much. I thought Bobby's ears were cute, like a cuddly teddy bear's.

"What are you talking about?" I said, irritated. "He is not ugly."

"Get over it, Jess," snapped Reese. "We're not all riding around as if we're at the Royal Show, you know."

"My name is Jessica," Jessica replied.

By this time we had arrived at the dressage area. Erica was waiting to start the lesson, and the conversation was over.

Erica raised her eyebrows when she saw how muddy I was. I explained that I'd fallen off.

The instructor looked thoughtful. "Just remember that presentation is important," Erica replied. Then she turned away to begin the lesson.

Erica began by asking us to push our horses into a trot. Despite my fall, I was glad I'd ridden to the grounds. At least I'd had some extra time to practice.

Erica yelled a lot. "Stop slouching, Annie." And, "Hold your reins shorter!"

I watched the others. Matt rode calmly, in a way that reminded me of the cowboys in old Western movies. Several times Erica had to remind him that he needed to keep both hands on the reins.

Austin and Reese both had very straight backs and a light way of holding the reins. Austin's horse, Cruise, was much taller than Jefferson, and she covered a lot more ground.

Jessica's horse, Ripple, had the most beautiful gaits. She seemed to glide around the arena in a lovely floating rhythm. Jessica, on the other hand, looked really stiff.

Jessica had bragged about Ripple's success at shows. I wondered how she did so well when she looked like she hadn't been riding much longer than I had.

"Ripple looks good," I called out to Reese. She was riding next in line behind me.

"Annie," Erica called out. "You can talk later. You really need to pay attention."

I turned red and quickly focused on Bobby. The constant nagging from Erica bothered me, but halfway through the lesson I realized that to my surprise, Erica's instructions were actually sinking in.

I felt great. My body was responding to the repeated commands. I was sitting up straighter, feeling more balanced in the saddle, and feeling more like Bobby's rider and less like his passenger.

At the lunchtime break, we all unsaddled our horses and made sure they had plenty of water and hay. Then Reese and I went to the lunch shed.

Mrs Moriarty and Mrs Coulson were serving the food. All of the parents were in casual clothes, which seemed right for a day spent with a bunch of horses. Except for Mrs Coulson, of course.

Just like the last time I had seen her, Mrs Coulson was dressed like someone from a magazine, with expensive-looking pants, a silk shirt, and lots of make-up.

I cringed when I saw her. I hoped Mrs Coulson wouldn't recognize me as the girl who had bought Jessica's old tack.

I took a ham and cheese sandwich and a squash. Then I paid for it and sat at a table with the others from my group.

"So how's your first day?" Austin asked before biting into a burger.

"It's great," I told him. "Bobby and I are having so much fun." I wasn't about to admit that I was kind of struggling.

Mrs Coulson was walking past the table and overheard. She turned to me. "Did you say Bobby?"

"That's right," I said. "He used to belong to Mrs Cameron."

"But he's a thousand years old. My goodness, I thought that horse had died!" remarked Mrs Coulson.

My hand shook, spilling squash from my plastic cup.

"He is really old!" said Jessica, who sat across from me. "And he's so slow. You should see him, Mum. He'd be laughed out of the show ring, that's for sure."

Then Jessica turned to me. "Not that you're going to show him. I mean, you'd need to update your tack first – it's all old and worn." She reached out and patted my arm. "But he's perfect for you. I mean, he's a great horse for a beginner. Much better for you to stick with a horse you can handle, isn't it?"

I felt like dumping the rest of my drink all over Jessica's perfect riding uniform.

The mention of the tack made Mrs Coulson remember me. "You're the girl who bought our old saddle!" she said, before returning to the kitchen.

Matt, Reese, and Austin all looked away, pretending to be very interested in their lunches.

Jessica smiled smugly. "I thought that tack looked familiar," she announced, looking pleased with herself.

I slammed down my cup. Squash splashed on to Jessica's perfect uniform.

"Hey! Watch it!" shrieked Jessica. I thought I heard someone nearby giggle.

"Sorry," I said. "I thought this was the riding club. I didn't realize it was a fashion show."

Jessica rose from her seat, glaring at me. "Whatever," she said as she left the shed.

"Jessica wouldn't know a good horse if it fell on her," Reese said. "The only reason she has Ripple is because her mother can afford to buy Jessica anything she wants. Besides, Ripple might be a good show horse, but even she can't make Jessica's riding look good in the jumping ring. Don't let her get to you."

But Jessica had got to me. After lunch, the lesson was games. Everything was new and unfamiliar, and I felt as if everyone was waiting for me to make a mistake.

So of course I did. In the bending race, I guided Bobby between the poles, weaving through them and back to Matt, who was waiting for me to pass the baton so he could begin his turn in the relay.

"Come on," Matt called eagerly. He held out his hand for the baton pass.

My hand opened a second too soon. The baton fell to the ground. Matt groaned. "Keep your eyes on it," he said. "Next time, don't let go until I grab it."

According to the rules of the game, I had to dismount and retrieve the baton before passing it to Matt. We were racing against the senior riders, and my mistake cost us. The other team raced ahead.

Then, in the two-flag race, I couldn't manage to get the flag into the small round hole at the top of the plastic cone. It took me three attempts, and by that time the seniors had won again.

"It's only practice," Reese consoled me, but the others seemed annoyed.

By the time the session was over, I had a headache.

Chapter Nine

I decided I'd had enough for one day. I removed my helmet, feeling instant relief as the breeze swirled around my damp, sweaty hair. Then I took Bobby to the paddock and unsaddled him.

I had to wait for Reese before I could go home, so I left Bobby with a water bucket and hay. With my head still throbbing, I leaned against the fence and watched while the others rode in the jumping lesson.

I felt a little better when I saw that Reese had been right about Ripple. When it came to jumping, Ripple didn't seem to know what to do, and Jessica didn't seem to know how to help her.

The horse didn't even jump when Joe, the instructor, put the jumps down so low that they were almost on the ground. Ripple would stop at the base of the jumps and then carefully step over them. Jessica tried kicking and even yelling, but Ripple wasn't the slightest bit interested.

"Jessica, yelling at Ripple is not helpful," called Joe from the side of the jumps area. "Horses don't speak English. All you'll do is scare her."

Jessica burst into tears. "But she's not even trying," she said, sniffing.

I couldn't hear Joe's response because just then, Mrs Mason walked over.

She told Joe to stop the lesson. "It's three o'clock, everyone," Mrs Mason went on. "But before you all go home, I wanted to let you know that there's a testing day coming up. If anyone wants to be rated for competition, or move up to a higher level, I'm taking names now. You'll be tested on the day to make sure your skill matches the level you want to compete at."

Jessica, who seemed to have recovered from her tears, had her hand up first. "I want to be graded for horse trials," she said.

Mrs Mason looked at her sceptically. "Are you sure, Jessica? I know your dressage is okay, but aren't you still having trouble with jumping?" she asked.

"I'm taking private lessons now," said Jessica. "I'm sure I'll be fine for D rating."

"Well," Mrs Mason said slowly. "D rating jumps are fairly small. I'll put your name down. But I won't rate you unless I think you're ready to try a competition."

Jessica shrugged, a smug look on her face. Jessica obviously thought she would impress Mrs Mason when the time came.

Austin, Reese, and Matt all put their names down. They wanted to be upgraded to higher levels. Mrs Mason looked at me, but I had no intention of putting my own name down. After today, I wasn't sure if I wanted to come back at all.

But before I had a chance to speak for myself, Jessica decided to do it for me. "Oh, Mrs Mason," she said. "I don't think Annie should be rated. She's not up to it. And she has such a long way to go before she'll be ready for a competition."

I stiffened. "Actually, I'll have plenty of time to practice, and I'm taking lessons, too. Put me down for D rating, please, Mrs Mason."

The second I finished talking, I felt sick. What private lessons? By the looks on everyone's faces, it was pretty clear they all thought I had lost my mind. And when testing day came around I would make an even bigger fool of myself.

Mrs Mason was the only one who didn't seem surprised. "I haven't had a chance to see you ride today, but I'll put you down. Same conditions as Jessica. Is that fair?"

I nodded. How dare Jessica accuse me of not being ready? She wasn't much better herself! I knew there was no way I'd back out.

Chapter Ten

The riding club grounds were almost empty by the time the ramp on the trailer had been raised into position, with Jefferson and Bobby safely inside.

We piled into Mrs Moriarty's 4×4 when I suddenly cried, "Wait! I mean, I'm sorry, Mrs Moriarty, but I left my helmet over near the games area. Can I just run and grab it?"

Mrs Moriarty seemed in a hurry to get home. "Hurry, please," she said.

I jumped out of the vehicle and ran to the games area. My helmet was still lying on the ground where I'd left it. I scooped it up and was about to return to the car.

Then I spotted Erica, the dressage instructor, waving and jogging towards me. Erica seemed bossy and a little scary. I wondered what on earth she wanted to talk to me about. "Annie! You're Annie, right?" she said when she reached me.

"Yes," I replied.

"I'm looking for help in my stable," Erica said. "You'd be required to work two or three days a week. When the summer holidays are over, you can come after school. I know you're inexperienced with horses, but if you want the job I'll train you. So, what do you think? Are you interested?"

I could see Mrs Moriarty watching me impatiently from the car. Then it hit me that

I was being offered a job. This could be my chance to earn enough money to buy new tack for Bobby and put an end to my dad's complaints about my expensive new hobby.

But, I wondered, why would Erica choose to offer the job to me? There were plenty of other people with way more experience.

Erica shoved a card at me. "Here," she said. "You can call me later with your decision."

Without another glance in my direction, Erica marched away. I headed back to the Moriartys' car.

When I mentioned that Erica had offered me a job, Reese and her mother exchanged odd looks.

"What's wrong?" I wanted to know.

Mrs Moriarty pursed her lips and said nothing. Reese, after a thoughtful silence, spoke up.

"It's just that Erica is known for, well –" she said.

"Reese!" Mrs Moriarty exclaimed. "Stop gossiping."

"Mum," Reese replied defensively. "Come on. We need to at least warn Annie about Erica."

Reese's mother was silent.

"What do you mean?" I asked, now alarmed. "What's she known for?"

"She's supposed to be really hard on her workers," Reese explained. "And she pays peanuts. Austin worked for her for a while, but he didn't last long. He said she expected too much of him."

"Well, I didn't say I'd do it for sure," I said. "I need to talk it over with Mum and Dad, anyway."

But the minute I arrived home with Bobby, my father appeared, waving a paper in his hand. He did not look happy.

"What is this, young lady?" he roared. I knew I was in trouble.

"Um, I give up," I said, trying to sound playful. "What is it?"

"Don't take that tone with me," my father barked. "I knew that horse was bad news. I didn't want you to have it in the first place. And now I'm getting bills for him!"

I was puzzled for a moment. Then I remembered the letter from Mrs Moriarty. It was still sitting on my desk. I had forgotten to tell my mother about the riding club fees.

I thought fast. "I forgot to give you the bill," I said. "Don't worry, I can pay it back."

"And just how are you going to do that?" he asked.

"I was offered a job helping at Erica's stables." *So much for buying new tack*, I thought.

My father calmed down a little. "You were?" He raised his eyebrows. "Well, now, that won't hurt you. I had a part-time job when I was your age. It's about time you started helping with the cost of all this horse stuff."

After I settled Bobby back in his paddock, I called Erica and told her I'd take the job. We worked it out so that I would walk to the stables, and my father said he would pick me up on his way home from work in the afternoons. So it was done. Tomorrow, I would begin my new job.

I tried not to think about what Reese had told me about Erica. The job would work out. It just had to.

Chapter Eleven

I arrived at Erica's stables a few minutes after nine the following Wednesday morning.

"You're late," were Erica's first words.

She handed me a broom and told me to sweep up the entrance area. Then she hurried off and I was left alone.

I looked around while I swept. The building was a huge brick and steel shed. At one end, where I worked, wooden stalls lined the walls on either side of a concrete aisle. The stalls were all empty, with the doors swung back against the walls.

I figured that the horses that lived in these boxes must be outside, enjoying the many small fields on the property. At the other end of the building was an Olympic-size indoor riding arena.

My eyes were drawn to the enormous ceiling overhead. Light streamed in through rows of skylights dotting the roof. Fixed between the skylights, a long row of electric light fixtures stretched from one end of the building to the other. I figured the long row of lights was used for riding after dark and in the early morning before dawn. Between the stalls and the arena was a horse-washing area and a few feed and tack rooms.

The walls of the arena stopped halfway up from the ground. This left an open-air window where horses and riders could see out to a brick-paved courtyard and spectators could view whatever was happening inside. At one end, a couple of small show jumps were set up.

A car and trailer arrived in the courtyard. I could hear the thump of hooves on the trailer's ramp as a horse was unloaded, but I didn't stop to see who it might be. I wanted to make a good impression by working hard on my first day, and that didn't include staring at the clients.

Everything was spotlessly clean, even the concrete floor I was sweeping, so it didn't take long for me to finish the job. I looked around for Erica, so that I could ask what I should do next.

Someone was riding a horse into the arena. I saw Erica walk over to the rider. It looked as if she was about to give a lesson. I decided it was better to interrupt now, rather than after the lesson started.

"Excuse me, Erica?" I asked, hurrying towards my new boss.

Erica, who had been talking to the rider, turned and looked at me. "Yes?"

"I finished sweeping. What should I do now?" I asked.

"There's a pitchfork and wheelbarrow in the feed room. You can start mucking out the stalls." With that, Erica turned back to her rider.

I had never mucked out a stall before, and I had no idea where to begin. I was about to interrupt for a second time when I caught the eye of the rider, who had been sitting quietly while I talked to Erica.

Suddenly, I realized that Erica had been talking to Jessica Coulson. She was watching me with a snobby expression. Surprised, and incredibly embarrassed, I hurried back to the feed room to find the tools I needed. There was no way on earth I was going to ask for help in front of Jessica. I would just have to do the best job I could.

Beginning at the first stall in the row, I set to work with the pitchfork, picking up dark green clumps of horse manure from the straw bedding. I could hear Erica shouting instructions to Jessica. The more I tried to focus on my work, the more my ears tuned in to Jessica's lesson.

After signing up to be rated, it was all I had thought about. Jessica had mentioned private lessons, but I had thought she'd been lying. That's what made me tell Mrs Mason that I was taking private lessons, too.

The problem was, now that I had this job, my riding time was limited. With more time to practice and private lessons, Jessica was sure to learn faster than me. When I showed up to be rated on the same day as Jessica, my riding was going to look pretty pathetic next to hers.

Maybe my father would let me have some private lessons, too.

I shook my head. No way. What was I thinking? I had no idea how much a lesson would cost. The reason I was working here in the first place was to help pay expenses. There was no way Dad was going to fork out even more money for private lessons.

Maybe I can listen in on Jessica's lesson, I thought. *I might be able to pick up a few tips to practice at home.*

Eavesdropping was harder than I had imagined. Erica used a loud, booming voice when she instructed, but I was still trying to clean stalls while I listened.

Then there was the problem of not being able to understand the words that I did catch.

Erica kept repeating, "Watch your diagonals." And then, "She's on the wrong lead, bring her back and start again."

I didn't have a clue what Erica was talking about. I finally gave up. I focused on shutting out the sounds from the arena and concentrating on the job at hand.

Later, when it was almost time for me to leave, Erica returned to inspect the stables. I was feeling pretty good about my work. Erica entered the first box. The straw had been neatly forked over and all trace of manure was gone. Smiling, I waited for words of praise from my boss.

Erica said nothing, but began kicking at the straw, lifting it up and away from the brick floor. Then I saw it. A large, smelly wet patch in the middle of the floor. I had been so busy listening in on the lesson and picking up manure that I had forgotten to check for urine.

Erica stared down at the telltale dark straw, looking thoughtful. I waited nervously. I knew how bad this looked. I was scared to hear what Erica was going to say. My first day on the job was probably going to be my last.

"Has anyone ever shown you how to clean a stall?" Erica asked quietly.

"No. But I didn't want to interrupt your lesson. I'm sorry. I'll stay back and redo them." As I spoke I could hear a car pulling up outside. It was probably my father, arriving to pick me up.

"Forget it," said Erica. "I'll give you a call if I need you again."

I was stunned. The job was supposed to be a real job, with real pay. And she had said she would train me.

Erica picked up the fork and dismissed me by waving me away.

I slouched in the front seat of my father's car during the drive home. Nothing seemed to be going right for me lately. I looked at my father, who kept his eyes on the road as he drove.

We would still be in the city if it wasn't for him, I thought bitterly. *I would still have all my old friends and everything would be so uncomplicated.*

* * *

That night, I called Jade. I was ready to have a nice long talk. I wanted to catch up on all the gossip I'd been missing.

Jade answered the phone herself. I could hear girls giggling in the background.

"Annie, hi," Jade said. "Listen, I can't talk right now, Lisa and Rachel are here. We're about to go see a movie. I'll call you soon."

I hung up and fell on to my bed. Even Jade was deserting me.

I got up and opened my wardrobe. I changed into a white skirt and a silver and blue top. It was definitely a city outfit. I hadn't worn it once since I'd moved to Ridgeview, because it didn't make sense in the country. But tonight it made me feel closer to Jade and my old life.

I pulled out a photo album. I slowly flicked through page after page. The photos, snapshots of my old life, were mostly pictures of me and Jade.

I gazed at a plastic-covered photo showing Jade and me in costume for the school play the year before. We were dressed as merry men, from Robin Hood's band. Jade had her arm flung loosely over my shoulder. We were both grinning like fools.

A tear rolled down my face and splashed on to the page. Somehow I knew that Jade and I would never be that close again.

Chapter Twelve

When I didn't hear from Erica, I was sure I'd lost the job at the stables. With no job and not much else to do, I was free to saddle up and ride Bobby. Together, over the next few days, we explored every bridle path we found in the country park. Bobby soon became used to the way birds suddenly flapped out of the trees, and he was no longer spooked by them. So we spent every day riding.

I felt better in the saddle now, but I still hadn't been able to ride faster than a trot. I had tried a couple of times to urge Bobby into a canter, but he didn't seem to understand. Instead of cantering, the old horse just stretched out his stride and trotted faster and faster, bouncing me in the saddle.

Then, one evening, after I had given up all hope of ever working in the stables again, Erica called. "I want to apologize, Annie," she said. "I was wrong to blame you for the dirty stall. I did promise to train you. You should always ask if you're not sure of anything."

"It's okay," I said politely.

"I would like you to come back to the stables and work for me. This time I'll train you, like I said I would. Will you come?"

I let out the breath I'd been holding. "I'd like that."

Erica sounded pleased. "All right, then. I'll see you tomorrow."

So I returned to the stables. Erica kept her promise to show me how to muck out the stalls. She explained to me that she had to keep the stables spotless, both for her own horses and the other people who paid money to rent stalls from her. Erica wanted everything to be done perfectly, and now that I knew what to do, my new boss expected me to have the stables perfectly clean all the time.

I also learned how to clean and oil tack. All the leather had to be kept soft, clean, and free of dirt.

I got really familiar with Erica's tack room. There were a bunch of bridles, several saddles, and various other bits and pieces. I had no idea what some of the equipment was going to be used for, but I carefully cleaned it all anyway.

I also learned how to use the washing machine to wash the sweat and dirt from a countless number of blankets and saddle pads. Then I hung them up to dry on a clothesline behind the arena.

And then there was the constant sweeping. Some days I felt like all I did was sweep.

Besides Jessica, a stream of other clients came to Erica for lessons. I would have loved to observe and learn from Erica's instructions, but with all the jobs I had to get through, there really wasn't time.

Still, there was one question that I really wanted an answer to.

After finishing my jobs on my third day of work, I looked for my boss.

"Erica," I said, following her into the riding arena. "Would you mind if I asked you something about riding?"

"I don't mind," Erica answered.

"I can't figure out how to ask my horse to canter," I admitted.

Right then, a rider came into the arena. I shut my eyes when I recognized Jessica and Ripple.

"You can't canter yet? You'll have to do that before testing day," said Jessica with a mean sneer.

Erica had been thinking. She opened her mouth to speak, but I quickly cut in, saying, "Um, I just remembered, I have to get home for something important. I'll see you tomorrow. Bye, Erica."

I hurried away.

After that humiliating moment, I couldn't find the courage to ask Erica about cantering again. The next time I saw Jessica at the stables was Saturday, the day before the next riding club rally.

I was just finishing up at the stables when I heard her voice in the arena.

"Yes, we decided to shave it," she was saying. "It's easier than having to plait it every time we have a show to go to. And don't you think she looks so much better?"

She must be having a lesson, I thought.

I wondered what Jessica was talking about, but there was no time to hang around and find out. I hung up the broom just as I heard my dad's car arrive to take me home.

* * *

As soon as I saw Ripple at the riding club the next day, I burst out laughing. Now the conversation I'd overheard made sense. Still laughing, I pointed to Ripple's tail.

"What happened to that?" I wanted to know.

Ripple looked really different from the last time I'd seen her. Her thick tail had been shaved at the top, almost to the tailbone. The hair at the sides had been plucked out altogether. To me, the tail looked unnatural.

"At least it's not ugly," Jessica said. "Like that!" She pointed to Bobby.

I swung around to look at Bobby's dark chestnut tail.

"What's wrong with Bobby's tail?" I demanded.

"Ripple's tail has been shaved and pulled for the show season," Jessica said. "If you knew anything about horses, you would know that. It's not a joke!"

I whispered in Bobby's furry ear, "If that's what it means to be a show horse, forget it. I'd rather see you looking real." Bobby flicked back one ear, as if listening carefully.

Jessica had another reason to show off, too. "Mum bought me a new saddle for the next show season. It's real English leather, and it's hand-stitched," she bragged. "She wants me to save it for special occasions, but I just had to use it today. It's so comfy."

I looked at Jessica's new saddle. I was really jealous of it. The saddle was beautiful, not that I would ever tell Jessica that. I looked down at my own scuffed and scratched saddle. Jessica's hand-me-down.

I knew exactly how expensive Jessica's new saddle would have been. It was going to take me months of hard work at the stables before I had anywhere near enough money for any brand-new saddle, and it definitely wouldn't be as nice as the one sitting on Ripple's back.

"Hey, Jess," called Reese, grinning at Jessica's annoyed expression. Jessica clearly didn't like her name being shortened. "Maybe you can talk Mr Snyder into giving a ribbon for the best-dressed rider on the games team."

Matt snorted, trying to hold back a laugh. Even Austin grinned. Reese seemed to delight in annoying Jessica, who was doing a pretty good job of ignoring me.

"At least I make an effort – and I can canter," Jessica retorted, looking straight at me before riding away.

I fought back tears. I had brushed and brushed Bobby's coat this morning. I couldn't make my tack look new, but I had stayed up late the night before to clean and oil it. And teasing me about cantering? That was just nasty.

"Ignore her," muttered Reese. "Her new saddle isn't going to help her to get Ripple over the jumps today."

Somehow that didn't make me feel better.

Riding in the dressage lesson with Erica felt weird. Now the instructor was here to help me, and not the other way around. Erica asked everyone to canter. I kicked at Bobby's sides, but as usual, I just couldn't make him canter. Erica was quick to see the problem.

"Annie, you're not asking him the right way. When you're asking for him to canter, stop rising to the trot, and sit your weight into the saddle. Put your outside leg back and push with your inside leg."

I followed Erica's instructions. When Bobby responded immediately by breaking into a rocking canter, I almost fell off in surprise.

"That's it, Annie!" shouted Erica encouragingly. "Now try it again."

By the end of the lesson, I felt a warm glow of satisfaction. Being able to canter on Bobby was a breakthrough. I was finally beginning to feel like a real rider.

Erica welcomed the junior group, Natalie, Bree, and Sophie, into the dressage arena as my group was leaving. Austin rode up beside me.

"So how's the job with Erica the Great?" he asked.

I turned to him in surprise. Austin had hardly spoken to me since I joined the club. The sarcasm in his voice annoyed me and I immediately defended my boss.

"Actually, she is great," I said. "I really like working for her."

"Are we talking about the same person?" Austin asked. "Nothing's ever good enough for Erica. Everything has to be perfect. I had better things to do than to be ordered around by her."

"Well, why did you take the job in the first place?" I asked. What was with this guy?

Austin seemed to suddenly lose interest in talking to me. He shrugged and rode off ahead.

I watched Austin go. He was so odd. He had hardly said two words to me before making fun of my boss. What an attitude! Maybe that was the real reason Austin hadn't kept working for Erica.

I worried about the jumping lesson. I had skipped it last time, but I couldn't keep doing that. Bobby seemed to sense that I was feeling more secure. He moved with a new spring in his step and seemed more eager to go than usual.

Joe recognized Bobby right away. "I know this horse," he said. "He'll have you jumping in no time."

Joe's words turned out to be true, at least from Bobby's side of things. We started off with poles on the ground. I was really beginning to feel good about trotting over the poles, but then Joe raised them on to stands.

Nervously, I watched the others take their turns.

Jessica seemed to have got something out of her lessons with Erica. Although Ripple still occasionally refused to jump, she mostly did as she was told.

When it was my turn to jump, Bobby's jump was smooth and steady. That didn't stop me from being thrown forward. I buried my fingers into the horse's mane and held on as best as I could. Somehow, I stayed in the saddle.

Joe asked me to ride a circle and go again. The second time was better, but the whole thing made my mouth dry up with fear. When Joe put the jumps higher for the others, I decided to stop jumping.

In the games lesson, Mr Snyder had set up a game that I hadn't seen before. Set roughly three metres apart, six poles lay in a row. The poles rested on small drums, leaving them raised about thirty centimetres off the ground, like a series of low hurdles, but closer together. Inside, I groaned. More jumping.

Before beginning, Mr Snyder explained a bit about the game. "This game is an excellent exercise to help you with your balance. It will really show who has the most obedient horse. The aim of this game is to jump through the poles, turn at the end, and jump back in the other direction. In a competition, the rider with the fastest time would win the game," he told the group. "Matt, you start."

Matt and his horse Bullet attacked the poles eagerly. The fast little horse bounced through the jumps in no time, spun at the end of the row, and bounced right back again. Matt made it look easy. Reese, too, steered Jefferson over the poles like a professional. But Austin said he didn't want to jump.

"Cruise is too big for this, and I don't want her to get hurt," he told Mr Snyder.

Matt's dad looked as if he was about to disagree, but then he just shrugged and waved Austin to the back of the line.

Jessica was looking at the poles nervously and didn't start her turn. "Ripple won't do it," she said.

"Give it a try," said Mr Snyder encouragingly. "This might be just what she needs."

Jessica nudged Ripple into a trot and focused her gaze on the obstacles before her. Ripple trotted right to the foot of the first pole. Instead of leaping over the poles, she crashed through the first two and then stopped dead. There was a clatter as poles and drums scattered.

"She's not even trying," Matt muttered from the watching group.

Jessica looked at Mr Snyder. "I told you," she said smugly.

Grim-faced, Mr Snyder started fixing the equipment. "Try it again," he told Jessica. "This time put some effort into it, and for goodness sake, look up! If you look down on the ground, then that's where you'll end up."

I could tell by the tone of his voice that Jessica had annoyed Mr Snyder. He was usually so patient. Jessica must have sensed it, too, because on her second try, she seemed to try harder. Ripple responded. They managed to clear every hurdle, although not very gracefully.

"That's better. A little more practice and that mare will be a great games horse," called Mr Snyder.

"Games is such a waste of time," said Jessica when she returned to the group.

Matt, who loved mounted games more than anything, immediately swung around in his saddle to confront her. "And prancing around in a show ring isn't?" he argued. "Maybe if you loosened up and had some fun for a change, your horse would, too."

Matt shifted his attention away from Jessica to me. "Go ahead, Annie. It's your turn," he said. Then he added, "I bet Bobby will be really good at this."

I eyed the course nervously. I thought if I could just hang on and let Bobby do the work, I might be able to get through it. I adjusted my grip on the reins, turned Bobby to face the poles, and weakly nudged his sides. The horse darted forward as if he were a racing car and someone had just dropped a start flag at Silverstone.

I was instantly unbalanced. My feet slipped out of the stirrups. I was half-hanging out of the saddle and trying to right myself when Bobby took the first pole, and then the second. In the short time it took him to arrive at the third pole, I felt myself sliding.

There was an awful crunching sound as I landed on the pole and then bounced on to the ground, banging my elbow against the metal stirrup as I fell.

Caught between one pole and the next, Bobby abruptly stopped, looking down at me like he was wondering what on earth had happened.

Mr Snyder was at my side right away. I sat up.

"Don't move," Mr Snyder ordered. "Did you hit your head? Can you move your toes?"

I blushed. Except for some bumps that I knew would turn into bruises, I wasn't hurt. Not physically, anyway. I closed my eyes when I saw Jessica smirk. Just when I'd thought things were finally coming together, I was back to square one.

"Bobby looks like he's done that before. It wasn't his fault you fell off," Matt said.

I knew that was true, and I didn't blame Bobby for the fall. But why did I have to fall off at riding club, in front of everyone?

Bruised and battered, I finished the day wondering again if I was kidding myself. Horses were much safer before, when they were only posters on my wall and part of my daydreams.

Chapter Fourteen

I was sure that signing up to be rated had been a horrible, serious mistake, and I even called Mrs Mason to ask her to take my name off the list. But Mrs Mason wouldn't let me back out.

"Don't take it all too seriously, Annie," she said. "It's normal to be nervous when you're learning to ride. The important thing is that you have fun. You are enjoying riding, aren't you?"

"Yes, of course," I said. Somehow I didn't think Mrs Mason would want to hear about my problems with Jessica.

"Well, keep practicing," she told me. "I know you'll put on a good show for me."

I hung up the phone and sighed. Adults always seemed to think they knew what you wanted, even when you didn't really know yourself.

The next time Jessica showed up at Erica's stables, I made sure I stayed far away from the riding arena. I worked inside the barn for the whole lesson.

Now that I knew the routine at the stables, Erica usually left me alone. She was busy giving lessons to a never-ending stream of eager riders, both children and adults. The only time I saw her that week was when she gave me my pay.

After she paid me, Erica asked me to do something new. "I was wondering if you would mind riding Bobby over here," Erica said. "I have a young horse to train, and I need someone to ride out with. Bobby is steady and quiet. He's perfect to help give this horse some confidence in a new environment."

So the next day I set out early and rode Bobby to the stables. Erica's young horse was a brown filly named Cadence. Before we had even left the property, Cadence had shied several times, and she was drenched from head to rump in a nervous sweat. Erica sat calmly on her back, not allowing the horse's unsteady behaviour to ruffle her.

It was the first time that I had seen Erica actually riding. She sat straight and tall in the saddle. Her hands on the reins were light and kind. Even to my inexperienced eye it was obvious that Erica was a practiced rider.

As we rode, Erica made comments on my position in the saddle.

"You're slumping," she said. "Sit up tall. Put your shoulders back and push your heels down. You should always ride in the correct position. The more you do it, the more it will become a habit."

Self-consciously at first, I followed Erica's instructions.

"Relax," Erica went on. "You're stiff as a board. Imagine if we swapped horses. How would you ride this one?"

"I don't think that would be a good idea," I said, eyeing Cadence's prancing gait uneasily. I hoped that Erica wasn't seriously suggesting that we swap. I was perfectly happy to stay on Bobby.

"That's exactly my point," said Erica. "You're lucky to have such a well-behaved horse. Bobby gives you confidence, but what if you had a nervous horse? Then you would need to give him confidence. If you don't relax, that won't happen. When things go wrong, it's usually the rider's fault. Even your quiet horse will improve as you do."

Easy for her to say, I thought, but I kept quiet.

Erica wasn't finished. "Look at your reins! They're all loose and sloppy." She shook her head. "Annie, you aren't riding this horse, not really. He's polite enough to let you sit on his back while he carries you around."

I began to protest, but Erica cut me off. "Why do you want to learn to ride, Annie?"

"That's easy," I said. "Because I've always loved horses and now I have Bobby."

"A lot of people love horses, but they don't all ride," Erica replied. "When I was your age,

I didn't have this wonderful opportunity that you've been given."

Erica looked at Bobby. "I had to scrape and beg and borrow," she said. "I would do anything just to get near a horse. Do you just want a horse to love, or do you want to become the rider I think you can be? Annie, how hard are you really willing to try?"

I wanted to point out that I had wanted a horse for longer than I could remember. And that now that I had a horse I was putting up with this awful secondhand tack and working hard – all so that I could learn to ride.

Oh my goodness, I thought suddenly. *I'm turning into a drama queen. I'm turning into Jessica Coulson.* Thinking over Erica's words, I realized that I had it pretty easy.

As an only child, I had my own space, I didn't have to share, and there always seemed to be enough money for extra treats.

In all the years that I had dreamed of owning a horse and riding, I'd just assumed that it would be easy, too, just like the rest of my life. Instead, it was turning out to be really difficult. And lately, I'd been feeling pretty sorry for myself.

I didn't just want a horse to love, although I loved Bobby. I didn't just want to prove to my father and Jessica – in fact, everyone else, too – that I could ride. It was more than that.

"Erica, I want to ride well," I said. "I want to be the best rider I can be."

I woke up the next day feeling good. My work at the stables had earned me almost eighty pounds. Another twenty pounds and I would have enough to pay my father for the riding club fees. After that I could start saving for a saddle. And tomorrow was the testing day!

After my talk with Erica, I had made up my mind to get serious. When I wasn't working at the stables, I rode. I wasn't going to let Jessica Coulson beat me. If practice made perfect, then

I would just have to practice, and then practice some more.

I had built myself a couple of jumps in the field. They were small, but I made myself take Bobby over and over them until I no longer felt that awful fear in my mouth.

Riding with Erica was helping, too. Each time we rode out together, I could feel myself improving. My rising trot was much better, and Erica had commented that my hands and seat were becoming lighter.

This morning, I had arranged to meet Reese at her house. We were going to run through all the things that Mrs Mason would be likely to ask me to do tomorrow.

Reese had a couple of very professional-looking show jumps in her field for practice. The jumps could be made higher or lower to fit different riding abilities.

Bright sunlight peeped through the cracks between the window and my bedroom curtain. I reached across to the window and pulled back the curtain, revealing the magnificent Japanese maple growing outside my window.

Beyond the tree, my eye sought out Bobby's field. I saw the sheep first. They were huddled in a corner, grazing, but I couldn't see my horse.

Then I spotted him. He was lying down near the gate. I smiled. I loved to see him with his legs tucked up beneath him and his head lightly resting on the ground. He looked like an oversized soft toy – especially the way his brown mane and tail contrasted with the red colour of his coat.

Sometimes I had to stop and catch my breath. It was still hard to believe he was actually mine.

Bobby suddenly stretched his forelegs out in front of him and tried to stand. The horse half-rose. Then he teetered for a moment before pushing himself up on all fours. As soon as he began to walk, I knew something was wrong.

"Bobby!" I screamed.

Still in my pyjamas, and not bothering with shoes, I raced outside to the field. Bobby was limping, badly.

I ran up to him. Quickly, I looked over his legs, then ran my hands down each of them one by one. They were clean, with no cuts or injuries.

I wanted to cry. Poor Bobby. What could be wrong? I had no idea what to do.

My mother came out to see what was going on. I stood with my arm around Bobby's neck. My feet were getting cold in the dewy grass. The bottom of my pyjamas had quickly become soaked, but I paid no attention to that. When I saw my mum, I burst into tears.

"He's limping, Mum," I sobbed. "I don't know what's wrong with him. What should I do?"

"The first thing you should do is go and get dressed, and put on some shoes," she said. "I'll call the vet." Mum took my shoulders and steered me back inside the house.

I tore my eyes away from Bobby. "I'm coming right back," I told him. "Don't worry, Bobby. We're going to make sure you're all better. I promise."

When Mum and I returned to Bobby, Dad followed. He watched with a nervous expression as I slipped a halter over Bobby's ears and clipped a rope to it. I knew he was thinking about the vet bill, but my concern for Bobby was bigger than everything else.

When the vet arrived, she drove her car right up to the paddock gate, got out, and shook hands with my parents.

"I'm Lydia Graney. What's the problem here?" she asked.

"Bobby's limping," I said tearfully. "I found him like this when I woke up."

"Let's take a look," said the vet. "Trot him out for me, please."

I took a firm grip on the lead rope and tried to coax Bobby to trot beside me.

"Well, he looks as if he's lame on both forelegs," Lydia commented when Bobby and I returned to her. "Hmmm, this could be serious, Annie. I can't see any external injury that would cause the problem. That could mean we'll have to do an X-ray."

Lydia started examining Bobby. First on one side and then the other, she picked up

Bobby's front feet. In her hand, she held a long-handled tool. It looked like a pair of tongs. Lydia used the tool to squeeze on each of Bobby's feet. Every time she squeezed, Bobby flinched in pain.

Lydia lowered Bobby's foot and turned to me. "It's his feet," she said. For some reason, she sounded relieved.

"What about them?" my father asked. I noticed an annoyed look cross my father's face when Lydia again turned to me.

"Have you been riding him a lot lately?" she asked.

"Yes, is that bad?" I asked, feeling panicky. What if I had done this to Bobby?

But Lydia shook her head. "Of course not," she said. "It's just that this horse has soft feet. Maybe he hasn't had a lot of exercise for a while."

"That's true," I said. "Before he came here he was just in a field with nobody riding him."

Lydia nodded. "Well, your problem is easily fixed," she said with a smile. "All you have to do is have Bobby shod, and he'll be fine."

"How much does that cost?" my father asked the vet.

"I can pay for it," I said. "I have a job. I get paid."

I avoided my father's stare. I knew what he was thinking. I still owed him the club fees. Now I would be in more debt than ever.

Just then, Reese arrived wearing riding clothes. She ran to me. "What's wrong with Bobby?" she asked. "Why is Lydia here?"

"Hello, Reese," said Lydia. "I'm leaving. Bobby doesn't need me. He just needs to be shod."

"Where can he have that done?" I asked Reese urgently. "It has to be done today so I can be rated tomorrow. I can't miss out."

Reese thought. "The guy who does Jefferson's shoes is out of town," she said, frowning. Then she brightened. "Erica! Ask Erica. With so many horses at her place, she'll know someone for sure."

Lydia agreed that it was a good idea. "Call me if you have any problems," she said.

As Lydia drove away, my father headed across the field to check on his sheep. My mother arrived and wrapped her arm around my shoulders. "Tell you what," she said. "I'll lend you the club fees. You can use your money to pay for the vet and for Bobby's shoes."

I smiled gratefully. "Thanks, Mum. Thanks a lot. But what will Dad say?"

"You leave your father to me," Mum said.

Chapter Sixteen

It was the testing day at the riding club grounds. I'd managed to track down a man who had been willing to come and put shoes on Bobby at short notice.

The shoes had worked like magic. In just a day, all traces of the problem were gone.

I watched nervously as Austin and Cruise approached their last jump. All the jumps looked enormous to me. This one was not only high but wide, too.

I still thought Austin was weird, but I couldn't help but admire him as a rider. He was by far the best in the group. Seeing him jump just made that more obvious.

Mrs Mason stood back from the course with a clipboard in her hand. She watched carefully as horse and rider soared over the last jump, cantered away, and then came smoothly back to a walk. Austin smiled at Mrs Mason as he approached her.

"Looks like you're up to B rating," she told him, smiling.

Matt, Reese, and Austin moved away to unsaddle. The three of them were happy. Matt and Reese had both been graded up from D rating to C, and now Austin was up to B rating.

That left only Jessica and me to take the test. I wondered again what I had been thinking when I had signed up for this.

I glanced across at Jessica, who held her horse by the reins. Ripple stood at her rider's side with head down and eyes half closed. My fellow D-rating hopeful seemed to be more interested in brushing herself down and repeatedly patting the bun of hair at the back of her helmet than in her horse.

I held on to Bobby while we waited our turn to show Mrs Mason our jumping skills (or, I thought sadly, more likely the lack of skills). The others moved away, leaving Jessica and me waiting for Mrs Mason. Finally, we were given the signal to mount our horses.

"I want you both to start by warming up at the walk and trot," Mrs Mason called. "Then show me your seat at the canter."

Before moving off, Jessica turned to speak to me. "Don't worry," she said. "Mrs Mason is pretty nice. She'll let you try again another day."

I didn't know whether to be offended or not. Jessica actually sounded as if she was trying to be nice. But she obviously still didn't think that I had a chance of making it today.

I was conscious of Mrs Mason's eyes on me. I tried to remember Erica's words. "Relax," she had said.

I nudged Bobby into a trot and concentrated on keeping an even rhythm. It was hard to focus. I glanced over and saw that Jessica had Ripple working nicely. I felt heat in my cheeks. I was sure I looked like a sloppy rider next to her. And I still didn't feel confident while cantering. Mrs Mason was definitely going to notice.

As if testing me, Mrs Mason suddenly turned up the pressure by calling, "Canter on."

Ahead of me, Ripple bounced into her usual showy canter stride. I sat down in the saddle, using my seat and legs to ask Bobby to canter, just as Erica had explained. It worked. Bobby loped around the ring. Relief flooded through me as I realized that I was actually doing okay. Maybe I could manage this after all.

Next was jumping. Thanks to all my practice, I was strangely calm. My biggest fear, that I would mess up the canter, was over with now.

But beside me, Jessica's cool expression began to slip. The other girl's hands were shaking. After my own recent experiences, I recognized the signs. Jessica's nerves were threatening to take over. I couldn't help but feel sorry for Jessica. And Ripple wasn't exactly a willing jumper, which made the job even more difficult.

"All right. You can go first, Jessica." Mrs Mason marked something down on her clipboard as she spoke. But Jessica suddenly couldn't ride.

"I feel sick," she mumbled. Her gloved hand clutched at her stomach and her lip curled.

"It's just nerves," I told her. "Think about something else."

But Jessica shook her head. "I can't," she said. "You go."

With a quick glance at Jessica, I rode out to ride the jumps. Maybe Jessica just needed more time. I tore my mind away from Jessica's distress and focused on the jumps.

I urged Bobby into a forward trot and approached the first jump. It was a simple crossbar and we cleared it easily. On to the next, a straight pole, then a double combination. I held my breath as I rode the course.

The last jump was the hardest. It was the same spread that Austin had ridden earlier, but lowered to be easier for less-experienced riders.

I looked ahead, willing myself and my horse to the other side of the obstacle. Clear!

When it was over, I trotted back to Jessica. The other girl still looked anxious, but at least she didn't look sick anymore.

"Go," I said. "If I can do it, you can, too. Just ride her into the jumps. Don't take no for an answer."

Unsmiling, Jessica nodded and walked Ripple slowly to the jumps.

Ripple stopped at the base of the very first jump. Jessica nervously looked up at Mrs Mason as if expecting to be sent from the grounds. But as Jessica herself had pointed out, Mrs Mason was kind. She waved a direction to Jessica to try again. Silently, I willed Jessica to get through.

She made it the second time and managed to ride the rest of the course without another stop. Mrs Mason called us over and told us her verdict. "You both have a lot to learn," she began.

Jessica and I exchanged looks. I could tell that we were both thinking that we hadn't made it.

Mrs Mason continued, "However, you have to start somewhere. You are both riding at the required standard for D rating." Mrs Mason tucked the clipboard under her arm and walked off towards the lunch shed.

A great sense of relief came over me. I turned to Jessica with a smile. "We did it!"

"I told you she was nice. She obviously felt sorry for you to let you through like that," said Jessica.

I stared in disbelief, then burst out laughing. "Right," I said, nodding through my laughter. "Whatever you say – Jess!"

I rode home through the woods, singing softly to myself. The trees closed comfortingly around us. Bobby plodded along with his head low and relaxed.

I couldn't remember feeling this happy in ages. It had been a summer of surprises and new experiences. The summer holidays would be over soon. My life would change again when school started. But even the thought of homework couldn't ruin my mood.

I leaned right over Bobby and hugged his neck as he walked. He smelled wonderfully horsey.

"Do you know what the best part of going to school will be, Bobby?" I asked him. The horse's ears flicked back briefly.

I dropped my voice low, pretending that Bobby was answering me. "No. What is the best part of going to school?"

"It will be coming home every night to you," I answered.

Bobby plodded on. He didn't argue. I told myself that was because he knew I was absolutely right.

About the Author

When she was growing up, Bernadette Kelly desperately wanted her own horse. Although she rode other people's horses, she didn't get one of her own until she was an adult. Many years later, she is still obsessed with horses. Luckily, she lives in the country, where there is plenty of room for her four-legged friends. When she's not writing or working with her horses, Bernadette and her daughter compete in riding club competitions.

Horse Tips from Bernadette

⊙ Horses are strong. Don't underestimate their strength!

⊙ You are your horse's most important teacher. Make sure that you're teaching your horse good habits, not bad ones.

⊙ Ride your horse with consideration. Never cause it pain.

⊙ Learn everything you can about horses.

For more, visit Bernadette's website at
www.bernadettekelly.com.au/horses

Glossary

⊙ **ability** skill

⊙ **bit** bar that goes in a horse's mouth and is attached to the reins

⊙ **canter** move at a speed between a trot and a gallop

⊙ **dressage** a method of riding and training a horse to perform

⊙ **girth** part of a horse's saddle that goes under its stomach to secure the saddle

⊙ **jodhpurs** trousers worn for horse riding

⊙ **obedient** well behaved

⊙ **occasional** once in a while

⊙ **paddock** enclosed area where horses can graze or exercise

⊙ **rigid** stiff and difficult to bend

⊙ **stirrups** rings or loops that hang down from saddles to hold riders' feet

Advice from Annie

Dear Annie,

There's this girl in my class who always picks on me. She makes fun of my clothes, cracks jokes about me behind my back, and is always starting rumours about me. I'm usually a pretty happy person, but she's really starting to get me down. What should I do?

Sad in Southampton

Dear Sad in Southampton,

I feel terrible that you're being treated like that! The first thing I want you to know is that this girl has a major bullying problem. But there are ways to defeat even the worst bully.

Here's how to get rid of a bully:

1. **Ignore her.** Bullies can only hurt you if you let them. If you don't pay attention, she might start to see that her words aren't affecting you, and she'll stop.

2. **Get help.** Some bullies just keep bullying, even after weeks or months of being ignored by their victims. If you've done your best to pretend she doesn't exist, but she's still bothering you, go to a parent, teacher, friend, or someone else you trust. Tell them what's been happening.

3. **Don't stop believing in yourself.** Those things she's saying? They're not true. Believe it.

4. **Don't bully back.** It's tempting to try to out-bully the bully, but it's not the right thing to do – and it won't make you feel better.

Good luck! Remember, no bully can ever take away who you really are. You're great!

Love,
♡ Annie

The Ridgeview Book Club Discussion Guide

Use these reading group questions when you and your friends discuss this book.

1. Jessica Coulson isn't at all nice to Annie – or anyone else. Everyone knows a real-life person like Jessica. What are some ways to handle a girl who treats everyone else like dirt?

2. Talk about Annie's relationship with her father. What are some of the feelings Annie has about her dad? How could their relationship be strengthened? What does each person need to do to make their family happier?

3. When Bobby gets hurt, Annie isn't sure what to do. More than one person comes to her rescue. Who helps Annie? Talk about the ways that different people can help you when you're in a tricky situation.

The Ridgeview Book Club Journal Prompts

A journal is a private place to record your thoughts and ideas. Use these prompts to get started. If you like, share your writing with your friends.

1. Write about one thing that you look forward to every day. Why is it so special and important to you? What would happen if you didn't have it?

2. Everyone surprises themselves sometimes, by achieving more than they expected or by being unable to do something they thought they could do. Write about a time you surprised yourself, either in a good way or a bad way. What happened? Why were you surprised?

3. Friendships are complicated, and it can be very difficult to begin a new friendship. Write about how your relationship with your best friend began. How did you meet? What did you think of your friend when you first met? How has your opinion of your friend changed?